POKÉMON™

POP QUIZ

POKÉMON

POP QUIZ

By Carli Entin

with Help from Professor Oak

SCHOLASTIC INC.

New York   Toronto   London   Auckland   Sydney
Mexico City   New Delhi   Hong Kong

There are more books
about Pokémon.

Collect them all!

Chapter Books:

#1 I Choose You!

#2 Island of the Giant Pokémon

#3 Attack of the Prehistoric Pokémon

#4 Night in the Haunted Tower

#5 Team Rocket Blasts Off!

Coming Soon

#6 Charizard, Go!

#7 Splashdown in Cerulean City

Also available:

The Official Pokémon Handbook

The Official Pokémon Collector's
Sticker Book

ISBN 0-439-15406-5

12 11 10 9 8 7 6 5 4 3 2 1   0 1 2 3 4 5 6/0

Printed in the U.S.A.

First Scholastic printing, January 2000

Table of Contents

Table of Contents

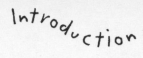

Welcome

to the Pokémon Pop Quiz!

I am Professor Oak. Many people consider me a Pokémon expert. I help new trainers get started on their Pokémon adventures. I trust you have been training hard, battling other trainers, and collecting as many of the 151 Pokémon as you can. You have probably been very busy learning everything there is to know about these amazing creatures.

But, how much do you *really* know about the world of Pokémon? Are you willing to put your know-how to the test? The Pokémon League has asked me to prepare a pop quiz and trivia book for Pokémon trainers to test their skills and train their brains. Included are almost 300 Pokémon brainteasers along with 26 amazing Pokémon facts!

The questions that follow come from all over the Pokémon universe. You will be quizzed on what you know about the Game Boy game, the TV cartoon, the first Pokémon movie, and — of course — the Pokémon themselves. Along the way, I will reveal secret Pokémon facts and let you show your stuff in special game corners.

By the way, the correct answers to all the questions can be found starting on page 73. There's even a key to rate your score and find out if you've got what it takes to become a Pokémon Master. But no fair peeking until you're done!

Well, it's time for me to get back to my lab. There is always more to learn about the world of Pokémon. And it's time for you to test your knowledge and have fun!

Ready, Set, Go!

How much do you really know about all 151 Pokémon and Togepi? Here's your chance to find out. In this book, there are fill-ins, true or false, and multiple-choice questions to answer. So, pick up a pen and go!

Name That Pokémon!

Which Pokémon . . .

1. is nicknamed the "gangster of the sea"? _____

2. spits flames hot enough to melt boulders?

   _____

3. has six tails and grows more as it evolves?

   _____

4. is the smallest Pokémon of all, at eight inches tall and only two pounds? _____

5. works in the Pokémon Center with Nurse Joy, nursing injured Pokémon back to health?

   _____

6. uses sprigs of green onion as miniswords?

   _____

7. stores thermal energy from the sun in its body?

   _____

8. can evolve into one of three different Pokémon? _____

9. drools nasty-smelling nectar when it thinks it is in danger? _____

10. triggers earthquakes by digging up to sixty miles underground? _____

11. is the pet of Giovanni, the head of Team Rocket?

   _____

12. lets loose its most powerful attacks when it gets a superstrong headache?

   _____

13. lives in caves and tunnels and uses radar to see in the dark? _____

14. has three coconuts for heads?_____

15. sleeps for eighteen hours a day, but can still use hypnosis while asleep? _____

16. has hooves that are ten times stronger than diamonds? _____

17. live underground in scorching molten lava?

   _____ , _____

18. carries an infant in its stomach pouch?

   _____

19. uses its spiky fins to swim backward?

   _____

20. has a jewel that glows with the seven colors of the rainbow? _____

21. uses its Barrier technique to build invisible walls?

   _____

22. whips its long tails during an attack?

   _____

Pokémon: Up Close and Personal

Look at these close-up photos of Pokémon. Can you name that Pokémon?

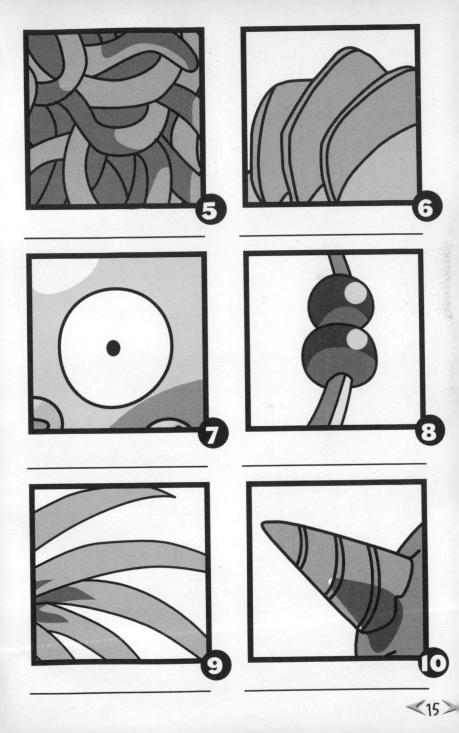

True/False

Some of the following twelve statements are totally true. Others are bogus. Can you tell which is which? Circle "T" for True or "F" for False after each statement!

1. In a battle, points are shared among all Pokémon who fought in that battle.   T   F

2. Pokémon cannot evolve in the middle of a battle.   T   F

3. Most Pokémon can only say their own name. T   F

4. Each trainer can carry up to six Pokémon at a time.   T   F

5. You can only collect one of each Pokémon.   T   F

6. Pokémon cannot escape from a Great Ball. T   F

7. Pokémon cannot escape from a Master Ball. T   F

8. In the cartoon show, Pikachu will never get into Ash's Poké Ball. T   F

9. Pokémon cannot die in battle. T   F

10. A wild Pokémon's health is automatically restored as soon as you catch it. T   F

11. Pokémon become more likely to listen to you as their experience increases. T   F

12. Once a person trades a Pokémon, he or she can never get it back. T   F

Know Your Pokémon!

The following questions are multiple choice.
Circle the correct answer.

1. Which of the following
   Pokémon does not evolve?

   A. Magikarp

   B. Rhyhorn

   C. Farfetch'd

   D. Seel

2. Which of the following Pokémon is not a
   legendary bird?

   A. Articuno

   B. Dodrio

   C. Moltres

   D. Zapdos

3. Which Pokémon does not
   evolve using a moon stone?

   A. Nidorina

   B. Clefairy

   C. Bellsprout

   D. Jigglypuff

POKÉ NOTE:
Snorlax is the heaviest
Pokémon, at 1,014
pounds! It's not pretty
when it wakes up on the
wrong side of the bed.
Luckily, it hardly ever
wakes up!

4. Which Fire Pokémon can hide in its own flames?

   A. Flareon

   B. Charizard

   C. Zapdos

   D. Magmar

5. Which of the following is not a real type of Poké Ball?

   A. Mega Ball

   B. Safari Ball

   C. Ultra Ball

   D. Great Ball

6. Which of the following techniques does not exist?

   A. Dragon Rage

   B. Seismic Toss

   C. Egg Bomb

   D. MagiKrush

POKÉ NOTE: Ditto can instantly turn itself into a mirror image of its enemy! Once it does that, it can use its enemies' powers!

Who's That Pokémon?

Name the Pokémon who . . .

1. lives in cyberspace and cannot be found in the wild.

   _____

2. is created from the Helix Fossil.

   _____

POKÉ NOTE:
Onix is by far the longest Pokémon, at twenty-eight feet, ten inches long! It would take more than twenty-eight Ditto or fourteen Sandshrew to measure up to Onix!

3. dips its tail in the water to become Slowbro.

   _____

Name the Pokémon that you can get by trading for a . . .

4. Jynx. _____

5. Mr. Mime. _____

6. Farfetch'd. _____

7. Lickitung. _____

8. Name the four Pokémon that won't evolve until they are traded through a Cable Club trade.

   _____ , _____ ,

   _____ , _____ .

POKÉ MATCH I

Match the Pokémon to its type. Draw a line connecting the correct pairing.

1. Fire

2. Water

3. Normal

4. Electric

5. Grass/Poison

6. Ice/Flying

7. Fighting

8. Poison

9. Ground

10. Flying/Normal

11. Psychic

12. Bug

13. Rock/Ground

14. Ghost

15. Dragon

A. Seadra

B. Caterpie

C. Mankey

D. Growlithe

E. Haunter

F. Lickitung

G. Golem

H. Drowzee

I. Dragonair

J. Oddish

K. Ekans

L. Raichu

M. Fearow

N. Sandshrew

O. Articuno

POKÉ NOTE:
Dodrio has three heads — one for joy, one for sorrow, and one for anger! And with three brains, you can bet it's one super-smart featherhead!

POKÉMON STADIUM 1

Let's face it — you wouldn't send a Bulbasaur out to do a Spearow's job. In other words, some Pokémon have the advantage over others in a battle. In the following battles, decide which Pokémon is likely to win, based on their elements. Assume that all the Pokémon have the same amount of hit points (or energy), and experience level. Then circle the Pokémon you think would come out on top!

1. Kingler vs. Rapidash

2. Haunter vs. Jigglypuff

3. Muk vs. Sandslash

4. Persian vs. Graveler

5. Moltres vs. Parasect

POKÉ NOTE:
Mew, Pokémon #151, can use every hidden and technical machine ever created!

6. Machop vs. Drowzee

23

In the Beginning . . .

The following questions are all about the beginning of you Pokémon journey. Write your answers in the spaces below each question.

1. In what town does the Pokémon game begin?

   _____

2. What is the one item stored on the PC in your house at the start of the game?

   _____

3. What item will Gary's sister give to you when you visit her house?

   _____

4. What is Professor Oak's relationship to your rival? _____

5. Name the three Pokémon offered to you by Professor Oak. _____ ,

_____ , _____

6. What does Professor Oak give to you in exchange for bringing him his package?

_____

7. What is in Professor Oak's package? _____

8. What is Professor Oak's nickname?

_____

9. What is Professor Oak's goal as a Pokémon scientist? _____

10. Who is the first person to challenge you to a match?_____

11. What are the boys on the television set in your house doing?

_____

12. Whose name does Professor Oak have trouble remembering when you first visit his lab?

_____

13. At the start of the game, who sent Professor Oak an e-mail to his lab?

_____

14. What does HP stand for? _____

15. What does PP stand for? _____

POKÉ NOTE:
When it rains, steam spurts from Charmander's tail.

Viridian City

Answer the following questions in the spaces provided. All are about Viridian City.

16. What does the Poké Mart worker give you on your way to Viridian City? _____

17. What are the names of the three computer systems at the Pokémon Center? _____ _____ , _____

18. Why can't you fight the local Gym Leader during your first visit to Viridian City? _____

19. What does it cost to nurse your Pokémon back to health at the Pokémon Center?

_____

20. Where is Professor Oak's package located?

_____

21. Where can you first battle with trainers other than Gary? _____

22. Who is blocking the path out of Viridian City when you first try to leave? _____

POKÉ MATCH II

Match the Gym Leader to the badge you earn for defeating him or her. Draw a line connecting the correct pair.

1. Giovanni   A. Marsh Badge

2. Erika   B. Cascade Badge

3. Brock   C. Soul Badge

4. Lt. Surge   D. Rainbow Badge

5. Sabrina   E. Earth Badge

6. Blaine   F. Thunder Badge

7. Koga   G. Boulder Badge

8. Misty   H. Volcano Badge

POKÉ NOTE:
Wartortle has huge ears that help it to balance when swimming fast.

Pewter City/Mt. Moon

All of the following questions are multiple choice. Circle the correct answer!

23. What can you find in the secret lab in Pewter City?

    A. Soda pop

    B. Moon Stone

    C. Old Amber

24. What skill does your Pokémon need to know to reach the secret lab?

    A. Dig

    B. Cut

    C. Roar

25. What type of Pokémon fossil can be found in the museum?

    A. Dome Fossil

    B. Helix Fossil

    C. Dome and Helix Fossils

26. What advantage does the Boulder Badge give you?

   A. Increases the special power of all your Pokémon.

   B. All Pokémon will obey you!

   C. Increases the attack strength of all your Pokémon and allows you to use Flash outside of battle.

27. Which two fossils are you offered after beating Team Rocket on Mt. Moon?

   A. Dome and Old Amber

   B. Helix and Old Amber

   C. Dome and Helix

28. How many floors make up Mt. Moon?

   A. Three

   B. Four

   C. Five

POKÉ NOTE:
Lt. Surge's nickname is "Lightning America"!

Cerulean City

All of the following questions are multiple choice.
Circle the correct answer.

29. How much will a new bike cost at the bike shop without a bike voucher?

    A. ₱1 million

    B. ₱1 billion

    C. ₱1

30. What advantage will the Cascade Badge give you?

    A. It will make Pokémon up to level 70 obey you.

    B. It will make Pokémon up to level 30 obey you and allows you to use the Cut skill outside of battle.

    C. It will make all Pokémon obey you!

31. Who is blocking the entrance to the bridge out of Cerulean City?

    A. Gary

    B. Team Rocket

    C. Snorlax

32. What will you receive for beating all six Team Rocket members on the bridge?

A. Dome Fossil

B. Helix Fossil

C. Nugget

33. What will the Pokémon collector give you in exchange for a Poliwhirl?

A. Poliwrath

B. Jynx

C. Starmie

34. What will you find in the Unknown Dungeon?

A. Mew

B. Mewtwo

C. Nobody knows! It's unknown!

POKÉ NOTE:
Graveler develop several layers of jagged scales that are chipped off in battle — and quickly replaced!

Vermilion City/S.S. Anne

All of the following questions are multiple choice.
Circle the best answer.

35. From whom can you get a bike voucher?

    A. Bill, the Pokémaniac

    B. The captain of the *S.S. Anne*

    C. The president of the Pokémon fan club

36. What will the Old Fishing Guru give you?

    A. A Magikarp

    B. An Old Rod

        C. A Great Rod

37. What is the advantage of having a Thunder Badge?

    A. Increases the speed of all your Pokémon and lets you use the Fly skill outside of battle.

    B. Increases the special power of your Pokémon and allows you to use the Cut skill outside of battle.

    C. Increases the speed of all your Pokémon and lets you use the Surf skill outside of battle.

38. Who gives you a ticket to board the *S.S. Anne*?

   A. Fishing Guru

   B. Bill the Pokémaniac

   C. Team Rocket

39. How often does the *S.S. Anne* visit Vermilion City?

   A. Once a year

   B. Once a month

   C. Once a day

40. Who is blocking the entrance to the captain's cabin?

   A. Gary

   B. Team Rocket

   C. Professor Oak

41. A Hidden Machine, or HM, is a new skill you can teach to more than one Pokémon. What HM, or Hidden Machine, will the captain of the *S.S. Anne* give you for helping him through his seasickness?

   A. Strength

   B. Fly

   C. Cut

POKÉ NOTE: Magikarp used to be known as a very powerful Pokémon, but currently it only knows one attack — Splash — and is not a very strong swimmer.

GAME CORNER 1: Evolution Mix-up

In the following groups, one Pokémon does not fit.
Decide which Pokémon is not part of the evolution.

1. Caterpie ———> Kakuna ———> Butterfree

2. Geodude ———> Graveler ———> Onix

3. Bellsprout ———> Weepinbell ——> Oddish

4. Abra ———-> Kadabra ———-> Arcanine

5. Paras ———-> Gloom ————-> Vileplume

6. Charmander ———> Wartortle ——> Blastoise

Celadon City/Lavender Town

The following questions are all about Celadon City and Lavender Town. Fill in your best guess in the spaces provided.

42. What Pokémon can be found in the Celadon Mansion?

_____

43. In the Game Corner, you will find a secret switch that will get you into the basement. Where is the switch located?

_____

44. Where do you get a Coin Case?_____

45. What do you need to get into Giovanni's office?_____

46. What will Giovanni give you for defeating him?

_____

47. What Pokémon is the ghost that is causing trouble in Pokémon Tower?

_____

48. What will Mr. Fuji give you for putting the trouble-causing Pokémon to rest?

_____

POKÉ MATCH III

Draw a line connecting the item to its purpose.

1. Poké Flute

2. Technical Machines (TM)

3. Silph Scope

4. Rare Candy

5. Lemonade

6. Thunder Stone

7. Hidden Machines (HM)

A. Restores 80 Hit Points to your Pokémon

B. Used to locate ghosts

C. Evolves Electric Pokémon

D. New abilities, given as rewards, that can be taught to more than one Pokémon

E. New abilities that can be found, bought, or won, and can be taught to only one Pokémon

F. Awakens sleeping Pokémon

G. Boosts experience level of your Pokémon

Saffron City

The following questions are multiple choice.
Circle the answer you think is correct.

49. Who is being held hostage by Team Rocket?

    A. Mr. Fuji

    B. Bill the Pokémaniac

    C. Silph Co. president

50. How many Gyms are there in Saffron City?

    A. None

    B. One

    C. Two

POKÉ NOTE:
Ninety-nine percent of a Tentacool is made up of water.

51. Which two fighting Pokémon will the Karate Master let you choose between as a reward for defeating him?

    A. Machop and Machamp

    B. Hitmonlee and Hitmonchan

    C. Machop and Hitmonlee

POKÉ NOTE:
Zubat live together in colonies in dark caves and tunnels.

52. What do you need to open the electronic doors in the Silph Co. building?

A. Lift Key

B. Card Key

C. Electric Pokémon

53. What is the advantage of having a Marsh Badge?

A. All Pokémon will obey you.

B. All Pokémon up to level 70 will obey you.

C. Increases the speed of all your Pokémon.

54. What will the Silph Co. president give you as a reward for beating Team Rocket?

A. Safari Ball

B. Master Ball

C. Poliwrath

POKÉ NOTE: Pidgeot can fly faster than the speed of sound, but Spearow's wings are so short, they struggle just to stay in the air!

55. What will the Silph Co. employee give you for beating Gary?

A. Lapras

B. Master Ball

C. Bike Voucher

fuchsia City

More multiple choice. Circle the correct answer.

56. Who will give you the Good Rod?

    A. Fishing Guru's older brother

    B. Safari Game Warden

    C. Misty

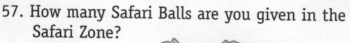

57. How many Safari Balls are you given in the Safari Zone?

    A. Thirty

    B. One Hundred

    C. One

58. Why can't anyone understand the warden of the Safari Zone when he speaks?

    A. He can only be understood by Pokémon.

    B. He lost his teeth.

    C. He says all his words backward.

59. What can you give the warden in exchange for the Strength skill?

    A. Fresh Water

    B. Any Pokémon caught in the Safari Zone

    C. Gold Teeth

60. What kind of Pokémon is waiting near the Power Plant exit?

A. Zapdos

B. Mew

C. Eevee

61. What skill will the reclusive Pokémon trainer at the top of the Cycling Road give you if you promise not to say where he lives?

A. Flash

B. Surf

C. Fly

62. What advantages will the Soul Badge give you?

A. Increases the attack strength of all your Pokémon and allows you to use Flash outside of battle.

B. Increases the speed of all your Pokémon and lets you use Fly outside of battle.

C. Increases the defense strength of all your Pokémon and allows you to use Surf outside of battle.

POKÉ MATCH IV
Match each Pokémon item to its purpose.

1. Poké Ball   A. Distracts opponent

2. Pokédex   B. Boosts defense rating

3. Poké Doll   C. Prevents random attacks

4. Repel   D. Used as identification

5. Carbos   E. Boosts speed rating

6. Dire hit   F. Used to catch Pokémon

7. Iron   G. Cures poisoned Pokémon

8. Antidote   H. Boosts attack effectiveness

POKÉ NOTE:
Dragonite are
supposedly as smart
as any human!

Seafoam Island/Cinnabar Island

The following questions are all about Seafoam Island and Cinnabar Island. Fill in your answers in the spaces provided.

63. How many levels are there in the Pokémon Mansion?

_____

64. Where is the secret key to the Cinnabar Island Gym located?_____

65. What Pokémon was created in the Mansion on Cinnabar Island?_____

66. Name the three extinct Pokémon that are resurrected from fossils in the Pokémon lab. _____,

_____, _____

67. What advantage does the Volcano Badge give? _____

POKÉ NOTE: Tangela is one of the shyest Pokémon around. You might be, too, if you were covered in seaweedlike vines!

Indigo Plateau/Ending

The following questions are all about the end of
your Pokémon journey! Fill in your best guess in
the spaces provided.

68. Name the Elite Four. _____,

_____, _____,

_____

69. Whom must you battle once
    you've beaten the Elite Four?

    _____

70. What do you receive upon
    collecting all 150 original
    Pokémon? _____

71. Which is the 151st Pokémon?

    _____

72. Where is Mewtwo located?

    _____

73. What advantage will the
    Earth Badge give you?

    _____

POKÉ NOTE:
Scientists created
Mewtwo out of the
DNA of the rarest
Pokémon on Earth
— Mew!

GAME CORNER II: Name the Element

Name the element that each group of Pokémon has in common. Write your answer in the space provided.

1. Magikarp, Krabby, Goldeen_____

2. Pidgeotto, Doduo, Scyther_____

3. Electabuzz, Pikachu, Voltorb_____

4. Oddish, Tentacruel, Beedrill_____

Episode Expert

The following questions are all about the Pokémon cartoon show, which airs on the Kids WB! network. How well you do on this part of the Pokémon Pop Quiz depends on how many episodes of the show you've seen. Gotta see 'em all to ace this section! Circle the correct answer to each question.

1. In the very first episode, who is the only Pokémon left when Ash finally gets to Professor Oak's lab to start his Pokémon journey?

   A. Bulbasaur

   B. Pikachu

   C. Squirtle

2. What is Ash wearing when he shows up to begin his Pokémon journey?

   A. Jeans and a T-shirt

   B. His pajamas

   C. A Haunter costume

3. All the police officers in the Pokémon world share the same name. It is . . .

   A. Jenny

   B. Joy

   C. Misty

4. All the head nurses at the Pokémon Centers share the same name? It is . . .

   A. Jenny

   B. Joy

   C. Suzie

POKÉ NOTE:
Diglett can move at 299,792,458 miles per hour!

5. After Misty "catches" Ash while fishing, why does she join his journey?

   A. Because she wants to capture Pikachu.

   B. Because he ruined her bike and she wants him to pay for it.

   C. To help him become a good trainer

6. What is Brock's goal?

   A. To make money to help his family.

   B. To become a great Pokémon breeder.

   C. To catch Water Pokémon.

7. What is the first wild Pokémon that Ash catches?

   A. Pikachu

   B. Metapod

   C. Caterpie

8. Meowth is supposedly the only Pokémon that can talk like humans. But in one spooky episode, this Pokémon also talks like humans.

A. Mewtwo

B. Pikachu

C. Gastly

9. Which of Ash's Pokémon was the first to evolve?

A. Caterpie

B. Pikachu

C. Charmander

10. What Type of Pokémon does Misty like to collect?

A. Water

B. Grass

C. Poison

11. In the episode when Brock, Misty, and Ash visit Mt. Moon, which Pokémon gather and pray around the Moon Stone?

A. Jigglypuff and Wigglytuff

B. Gloom and Vileplume

C. Clefairy and Clefable

12. Jessie and James want to capture one of Ash's Pokémon. Which one?

   A. Metapod

   B. Charmander

   C. Pikachu

13. What is the name of the school for Pokémon trainers who want to join the Pokémon League but do not go on a journey to collect badges and catch wild Pokémon?

   A. Pokémon University

   B. Pokémon Tech

   C. Pokémon College

14. In the Vermilion City Gym, Ash's Pikachu is able to beat Lt. Surge's Raichu, an evolved form of Pikachu. Why?

   A. Raichu evolved too quickly — before learning important skills.

   B. Pikachu had help from Ash's Butterfree.

   C. Raichu was weakened by an electric cold.

15. Which Pokémon started a gang after being abandoned by their trainers?

   A. Squirtle

   B. Bulbasaur

   C. Raticate

16. When Ash catches a Krabby, it is sent to stay with Professor Oak. Why?

   A. Professor Oak had never seen a Krabby and wanted to study it.

   B. Ash could only carry six Pokémon at a time, and Krabby would have been his seventh.

   C. The Krabby was a fake.

17. How can Ash exchange the Pokémon he carries with him for one being looked after by Professor Oak?

   A. By traveling to Pallet Town and accessing his computer.

   B. By pressing the white button inside his Pokédex.

   C. By having Professor Oak mail him his Pokémon.

POKÉ NOTE: According to Misty, the three most disgusting things in the world are peppers, carrots, and bugs — like Caterpie!

18. While aboard the *S.S. Anne*, what kind of Pokémon does Ash trade his Butterfree for?

A. Raticate

B. Rattata

C. Nidoran

19. Also aboard the *S.S. Anne*, what kind of Pokémon does James spend all of his money on?

A. Goldeen

B. Horsea

C. Magikarp

20. Which Pokémon does Ash release into the wild to find a mate?

A. Butterfree

B. Caterpie

C. Pikachu

21. Which Pokémon won a battle for Ash by making the Gym Leader Sabrina laugh at the Saffron City Gym?

A. Gastly

B. Gengar

C. Haunter

22. Name the Hypno-induced illness that makes people think they are Pokémon.

   A. Poké Pox

   B. Pokémonitis

   C. Poké Fever

POKÉ NOTE: Hypno carries around a special pendant to put its opponents to sleep!

23. While under a spell in Hop-hop-hop City, which Pokémon does Misty think she is?

   A. Horsea

   B. Starmie

   C. Seel

24. Which Pokémon does Misty accidentally catch when her Poké Ball gets loose?

   A. Seadra

   B. Goldeen

   C. Psyduck

25. At the lighthouse, what kind of Pokémon was Bill, the Pokémon researcher, dressed up as?

   A. Kabuto

   B. Kingler

   C. Fearow

26. What ability of Gyarados
    do sailors fear?

    A. Hyper Pump

    B. Dragon Rage

    C. Hyper Beam

27. Why was Tentacruel so angry
    with the people of Porta Vista?

    A. It was awakened from its hibernation.

    B. Its ocean home was being destroyed.

    C. It did not want to be caught in a Poké Ball.

28. Which two Pokémon did Gastly combine into
    one while it was pretending to be the ghost of
    Maiden's Peak?

    A. Venasaur and Blastoise, into Venustoise

    B. Hypno and Seadra, into Hypra

    C. Gengar and Pikachu, into Gengachu

29. What perfume did Jessie and James steal from
    Erika in Celadon City?

    A. Eau de Vileplume

    B. Essence of Gloom

    C. Persian Perfume

30. In an early episode, why was Magnemite so attracted to Pikachu?

A. Pikachu saved it from some angry Muk.

B. Pikachu had a cold, and had a lot of electric energy stored in its cheeks.

C. Magnemite wanted to steal Pikachu's energy and use it to evolve into Magneton.

POKÉ NOTE:
Charmander may look little, but its Rage Attack packs a punch! Rage allows Charmander to build up anger into one powerful attack. Ash's Charmander used Rage Attack to catch a wild Primeape!

31. Which of Ash's Pokémon was left with Anthony, the Fighting Pokémon trainer, after Primeape won the Grand Prix competition?

A. Primeape

B. Hitmonlee

C. Machop

32. In one episode, Brock, Ash, and Misty come to a town that has no water, and therefore can't grow food. What is the problem?

A. Team Rocket vacuumed all the water out of the town.

B. A group of Tentacruel stole all the water for their colony.

C. A sleeping Snorlax was blocking the water supply.

33. Ash once made up a fake name so that he could fight ninjas and not be recognized. What was it? Hint: He was looking at a bottle of ketchup at the time.

A. Red Bottle

B. Tom Ato

C. Ash Ketchup

34. What were Ash, Misty, and Brock taking to Sunny Town when they were stopped by the bridge bike gang?

A. Bikes

B. Medicine for a sick Pokémon

C. Pikachu, to the Pokémon Center

35. What was wrong with the Ditto that belongs to a millionairess from the House of Imitay?

A. It couldn't reproduce the faces of the Pokémon it copied.

B. It couldn't reproduce the attacks of the Pokémon it copied.

C. It couldn't reproduce the defenses of the Pokémon it copied.

36. What Pokémon did little Mikey, a boy from Stone Town, decide to evolve his Eevee into?

POKÉ NOTE:
The chef at one restaurant Ash and friends stop in loves Psyduck so much, he'll give you a free meal if you have one!

A. Vaporeon

B. Jolteon

C. He decided not to evolve his Eevee.

37. While taking a break in the forest, why does Ash want to leave Pikachu behind?

A. He is angry that Pikachu won't obey him and get in the Poké Ball.

B. He wants to experiment with using other Pokémon.

C. He wants Pikachu to live free among a group of wild Pikachu.

38. What do people dig for in Grandpa Canyon?

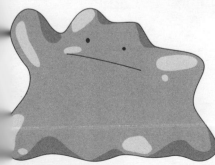

A. Gold

B. Fossils

C. Rare Pokémon

POKÉ NOTE:
Sweet dreams give Drowzee and Hypno energy. Bad dreams make them sick!

WHO'S MY TRAINER?

Each group of three Pokémon has the same trainer. Name the character from the cartoon that trains all three. Write the names in the spaces below.

_____1. Pikachu   Butterfree   Krabby

_____2. Goldeen   Horsea   Psyduck

_____3. Geodude   Vulpix   Onix

_____4. Koffing   Victreebel   Magikarp

39. Why does Paras's trainer, Cassandra, want it to evolve into Parasect?

A. So it will be stronger in battle.

B. To make a special potion out of Parasect's mushroom.

C. To prove to her family that she is a good trainer.

40. Which Pokémon does Misty leave at the breeding center run by Butch and Cassidy?

A. Psyduck

B. Starmie

C. Horsea

41. What kind of Pokémon was James's pet when he was a boy?

A. Growlithe

B. Arcanine

C. Pikachu

42. Which of Ash's Pokémon did not want to evolve with the rest of its kind?

A. Charmander

B. Pikachu

C. Bulbasaur

43. In the episode where Ash takes a written Pokémon League test, who gets expelled from the Admissions Center?

A. Ash

B. Misty

C. Jessie

44. Who won the title "Queen of the Princess Festival"?

A. Jessie

B. Misty

C. Ash's mother

POKÉ NOTE:
Jessie and James are so bad at capturing Pokémon, they claim to have CFS — Chronic Failure Syndrome!

45. Blaine is the Gym Leader on Cinnabar Island. He likes to test trainers with tough riddles. What does he say is "read," but has no words?

A. Misty's hair

B. Volcano Badge

C. A Pokédex

46. Who is the turtle Pokémon king?

A. Squirtle

B. Blastoise

C. Wartortle

47. What kind of Pokémon is part of a special K-9 police unit?

A. Arcanine

B. Persian

C. Growlithe

48. When Misty assisted Melvin the Magician with his failing festival act, Melvin put a spell on Ash! Which Pokémon did he use?

A. Exeggute

B. Exeggutor

C. Jynx

49. In a later episode, these Pokémon stole things to build a rocket.

A. Clefairy

B. Clefable

C. Jigglypuff

50. Jessie and James thought they had finally caught a rare Pokémon when they snatched a Mr. Mime at Misty's Gym. What did they really catch?

A. Ash, dressed as Mr. Mime

B. Misty, dressed as Mr. Mime

C. A Mr. Mime stuffed animal

51. Who did Ash have to beat to get his Earth Badge?

A. Giovanni

B. Team Rocket's Jessie and James

C. Sabrina

52. Who is the ringmaster of the Pokémon circus?

   A. Stella

   B. Merlin

   C. Brock

53. Which Pokémon act as "Santa's Helpers"?

   A. Porygon

   B. Rapidash

   C. Jynx

54. Which Pokémon helps Ash's mother around the house?

   A. Mr. Mime

   B. Pikachu

   C. Persian

55. At the Pallet Town nursery, why wouldn't the leaf stone work on Florinda's Gloom?

A. Gloom wasn't gloomy enough.

B. Florinda's leaf stone was fake.

C. Gloom didn't have enough battle experience.

56. Ash and his friends find a Jigglypuff in Neon City who will not sing. Why not?

A. It was weakened by a fight with Team Rocket.

B. It didn't know how to sing.

C. It was too shy to sing.

POKÉ NOTE: Rapidash will race almost anyone! Ash races on one after its trainer, Laura, is injured.

POKÉ MATCH V

Match the character on the Pokémon TV show to his or her description.

1. Nastina

A. Runs a gym not sponsored by the Pokémon League.

2. A.J.

B. Decided to train Grass Pokémon because a Gloom saved her from a Grimer's attack.

3. Sabrina

C. Takes pictures of wild Pokémon. Team Rocket wanted this person to capture Pikachu, and he did — on film!

4. Erika

5. Todd

D. Turned Ash, Brock, and Misty into dolls.

E. Wanted to get rid of all the Tentacool in Porta Vista and build a resort there.

Map It!

Think you can find your way around the Pokémon Universe? It can't be easy, since Ash, Brock, Misty, and Team Rocket are often lost!

1. _____
_____

2. _____
_____

3. _____
_____

4. _____
_____

5. _____
_____

6. _____
_____

7. _____
_____

8. _____
_____

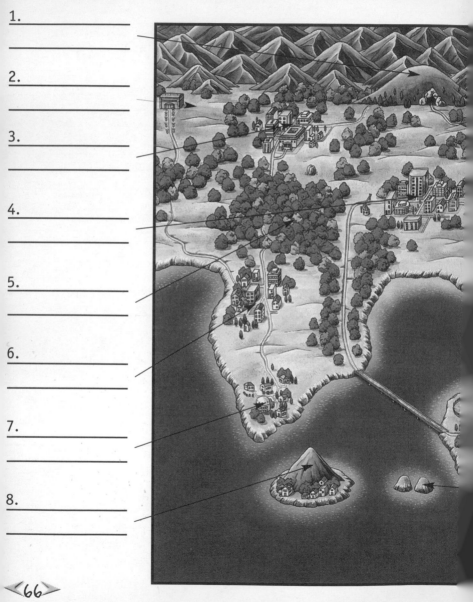

Fill in the names of cities, forests, and islands on this map to see how you would do as a trainer in the wild!

9. _____

_____

10. _____

_____

11. _____

_____

12. _____

_____

13. _____

_____

14. _____

_____

15. _____

_____

Which Human Character . . .

1. won an official Pokémon League hat that was then stolen by a Primeape? _____

2. does most of the cooking for Ash, Misty, and Brock? _____

3. came from a wealthy family who wanted him to marry "Jessebelle"? _____

4. thought Santa Claus stole her favorite doll?
   _____

5. joined Ash and Misty on their journey after Brock decided to stay on the Orange Islands?
   _____

6. was talked into starring in an underwater dance recital? _____

7. won the trophy for excellence three years running at the World Pokémon Breeders' contest? _____

8. treated Pikachu when it had an apple stuck in its throat? _____

9. stole other people's Pokémon because he didn't think his Farfetch'd was good enough to catch wild Pokémon? _____

10. took a job as a Gym Leader because he didn't want to leave his brothers and sisters?

_____

11. was saved from a bunch of wild Zubat on Mt. Moon? _____

12. can disguise herself to look like any other person, much like her Ditto?

_____

<69>

Pokémon Stadium II:
And the Winner Is...

Ash and his friends have picked up a lot of Pokémon on their journey! Based on Type, decide which Pokémon would win the following battles. Assume that each Pokémon is at the same experience level.

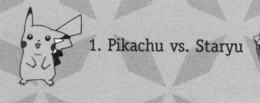

1. Pikachu vs. Staryu

2. Geodude vs. Charmander

3. Psyduck vs. Primeape

4. Arbok vs. Onix

5. Horsea vs. Gloom

6. Vulpix vs. Caterpie

At the Movies

The following questions are all about the Pokémon movie, *Mewtwo Strikes Back,* and the short movie *Pikachu's Vacation.* These are multiple choice, so circle the correct answer!

PIKACHU'S VACATION

1. What is Pikachu's responsibility at the Playground?

   A. To get along with the other Pokémon.

   B. To look after Ash, Misty, and Brock's other Pokémon—especially Togepi.

   C. To stay out of trouble.

2. Why do the rest of the Pokémon need to help Charizard?

   A. It doesn't know how to have fun.

   B. It is about to fall off a cliff.

   C. Its head is stuck in a pipe.

POKÉMON THE FIRST MOVIE: MEWTWO STRIKES BACK

3. Who were the scientists that created Mewtwo working for?

   A. Professor Oak

   B. The Pokémon League

   C. Giovanni

4. What is the name of the deadly storm created by Mewtwo?

    A. Ocean's Rage

    B. Tide of Terror

    C. Winds of Water

5. What does Mewtwo do with the Pokémon it takes away from their trainers?

    A. Destroy them.

    B. Use their DNA to make clones.

    C. Turn them against their original trainers.

6. Why does Mewtwo want to destroy all Pokémon?

    A. Mewtwo thinks that Pokémon have disgraced themselves by serving humans.

    B. Mewtwo thinks that the other Pokémon are out to destroy it.

    C. Mewtwo doesn't want to destroy Pokémon.

7. What lesson does Mewtwo learn from its mistakes?

    A. Pokémon can never be destroyed.

    B. Life is what you make it — no matter where you come from.

    C. Humans can't be trusted.

POKÉ NOTE:
What Attacks will Togepi have when it grows up? It's a mystery. Misty's guess is Teleport and Metronome. While on the Island of the Pink Pokémon, Misty and her friends were saved by a Teleport Attack and one like Barrier. But who saved them? Could it have been Togepi?

ANSWERS

<u>WARNING!</u> You have just entered the No Peeking Zone — unless, of course, you're all done taking the Pop Quiz.

Hello again! Professor Oak here!

So, how'd you do? Check out the answers below to see how you scored. Count up how many questions you got right to see if becoming a Pokémon Master is your destiny.

Name That Pokémon!
(pages 8–9)

1. Tentacruel
2. Charizard
3. Vulpix
4. Diglett
5. Chansey
6. Farfetch'd
7. Dewgong
8. Eevee
9. Gloom
10. Dugtrio
11. Persian
12. Psyduck
13. Zubat
14. Exeggutor
15. Abra
16. Ponyta
17. Rhydon and Magmar
18. Kangaskhan
19. Seadra
20. Starmie
21. Mr. Mime
22. Tauros

Pokémon: Up Close and Personal (pages 10–11)

1. Poliwag
2. Onix
3. Electrode
4. Weezing
5. Tangela
6. Machoke
7. Magnemite
8. Dragonair
9. Exeggutor
10. Rhydon

True/False (page 18)

1. T
2. F
3. T
4. T
5. F
6. F
7. T
8. T
9. T
10. F
11. F
12. F

Know Your Pokémon! (pages 19–20)

1. C

2. B
3. C
4. D
5. A
6. D

Poké Match I (page 21)

1. D
2. A
3. F
4. L
5. J
6. O
7. C
8. K
9. N
10. M
11. H
12. B
13. G
14. E
15. I

Who's That Pokémon? (page 22)

1. Porygon
2. Omanyte
3. Slowpoke
4. Poliwhirl

5. Abra
6. Spearow
7. Slowpoke
8. Alakazam, Golem, Machamp, Gengar

Pokémon Stadium I
(page 23)

1. Kingler
2. Jigglypuff
3. Muk
4. Graveler
5. Moltres
6. Drowzee

In the Beginning . . .
(pages 24–26)

1. Pallet Town
2. Potion
3. Town map
4. Grandfather
5. Bulbasaur, Charmander, Squirtle
6. Pokédex
7. A special Poké Ball
8. Pokémon Prof
9. To make a database of all the Pokémon in the world

10. Gary
11. Walking on railroad tracks
12. Gary's
13. Elite Trainers of Pokémon League
14. Hit points
15. Power points

Viridian City
(page 27)

16. Potion
17. Your PC, Bill's PC, Oak's PC
18. The gym's doors are locked
19. Nothing — it's free!
20. At the Viridian City Poké Mart
21. Viridian Forest
22. A grumpy old man

Poké Match II
(page 28)

1. E
2. D
3. G
4. F
5. A
6. H

7. C
8. B

Pewter City/Mt. Moon
(pages 29–30)

23. C
24. B
25. A
26. C
27. C
28. A

Cerulean City
(pages 31–32)

29. A
30. B
31. A
32. C
33. B
34. B

Vermilion City/
S.S. Anne (pages 33–34)

35. C
36. B
37. A
38. B
39. A
40. A
41. C

Game Corner I: Evolution
Mix-up (page 35)

1. Kakuna
2. Onix
3. Oddish
4. Arcanine
5. Paras
6. Charmander

Celadon City/
Lavender Town
(page 36)

42. Eevee
43. Behind the poster
44. At the diner
45. Lift key
46. Sith scope
47. Marowak
48. Poké Flute

Poké Match III
(page 37)

1. F
2. E
3. B
4. G
5. A
6. C
7. D

Saffron City
(pages 38–39)

49. C
50. C
51. B
52. B
53. B
54. B
55. A

Fuchsia City
(pages 40–41)

56. A
57. A
58. B
59. C
60. A
61. C
62. C

Poké Match IV
(page 42)

1. F
2. D
3. A
4. C
5. E
6. H
7. B
8. G

Seafoam Island/ Cinnabar Island
(page 43)

63. Four
64. In the Pokémon Mansion basement
65. Mewtwo
66. Omanyte, Kabuto, Aerodactyl
67. Increases special power of all your Pokémon

Indigo Plateau/Ending
(page 44)

68. Lorelei, Agatha, Bruno, Lance
69. Gary
70. A certificate
71. Mew
72. Unknown Dungeon
73. All Pokémon will obey you!

Game Corner II: Name the Element (page 45)

1. Water
2. Flying
3. Electric
4. Poison

Episode Expert
(pages 46–64)

1. B
2. B
3. A
4. B
5. B
6. B
7. C
8. C
9. A
10. A
11. C
12. C
13. B
14. A
15. A
16. B
17. B
18. A
19. C
20. A
21. C
22. B
23. C
24. C
25. A
26. B
27. B
28. A
29. B
30. B
31. A
32. C
33. B
34. B
35. A
36. C
37. C
38. B
39. B
40. A
41. A
42. C
43. C
44. B
45. B
46. B
47. C
48. A
49. A
50. A
51. B
52. A
53. C
54. A
55. B
56. B

Who's My Trainer?
(page 58)

1. Ash
2. Misty
3. Brock
4. James

Poké Match V
(page 65)

1. E
2. A
3. D
4. B
5. C

Map It! (pages 66–67)

1. Mt. Moon
2. Indigo Plateau
3. Pewter City
4. Celadon City
5. Viridian Forest
6. Viridian City
7. Pallet Town
8. Cinnabar Island
9. Sea Cottage
10. Cerulean City
11. Lavender Town
12. Saffron City
13. Vermilon City
14. Fuchsia City
15. Seafoam Islands

Which Human Character . . .
(pages 68–69)

1. Ash
2. Brock
3. James
4. Jessie
5. Tracy
6. Misty
7. Susan
8. Dr. Proctor
9. Keith
10. Brock
11. Seymour
12. Duplica

Pokémon Stadium II: And the Winner Is . . .
(page 70)

1. Pikachu
2. Geodude
3. Psyduck
4. Onix
5. Gloom
6. Vulpix

At the Movies
(pages 71–72)

1. B
2. C
3. C
4. C
5. B
6. A
7. B

So, are you the master trainer you thought you were? Count up the number of questions you got right to find out. There were over 300 questions in all. The more questions you answered correctly, the more you score.

Scoring Chart

1–50 = POKÉMON NOVICE
Pack up your Poké Balls and head for home. You'll need to study hard before you will be ready to take on a wild Pokémon. But don't worry, you can do it!

51–100 = JUNIOR TRAINER
Just starting out? No worries. Study hard and practice, practice, practice! You are guaranteed to improve.

101–150 = OAK'S ASSISTANT
You've got the smarts, now let's see you put them to use. To catch and train wild Pokémon will be your real test. Search far and wide. You are on the right track.

151–200 = GYM LEADER
You are unstoppable! Keep up the good work. There are many Pokémon victories in your future.

OVER 200 = POKÉMON MASTER
To be a Pokémon Master is your destiny.